Collect My Dust

by

Dana Rodney

Tragic/Comic Poems of a Newly Old Woman

The following poems were written during the years 2017-2023 during which I retired accidentally, two homes burned down in California wildfires, I reluctantly turned sixty, and struggled with the rest of the world through the COVID pandemic. At least sheltering-in-place was a good opportunity to hunker down and write some poems.

True to my personality and the ups and downs of those years, these poems fluctuate from comic to tragic. Maybe you'll smile and cry along with me as you read them.

Your book reviews on Amazon are truly appreciated!

I'd love to hear from you. Please write and let me know which poems were your favorites at: danarodneybiz@gmail.com.

More at my website: danarodney.com.

Contents

Inspired by an award-winning documentary
from Spain called "A Hundred Days of Solitude"
by Jose Diaz.

At This Very Moment

I cannot abide abiding here,
inside my mind's old home behind my eyes,
seeing only what my eyes can see,
confined only to places
my body brings me.

When I am certain
at this very moment
the roan deer are galloping
across the snowy peaks of northern Spain,
and violet swallows are building nests
in silent desert canyons.
Snow is falling softly in Nepal
on the brows of monkeys
huddled in pine trees,
and waves are crashing in Patagonia
grinding stones into sand.
Massive pods of humpback whales
are gliding unseen beneath the ocean,
and uncountable trees are sleeping patiently
in the frozen north
blanketed in snow.

4

But also,
at this very moment,
a newborn baby
abandoned on the thorny ground
is whimpering too softly to hear,
and a suicidal girl is clutching
the railing of a bridge somewhere.

And sometimes I am the whale
gliding effortlessly,
and I am the tree hunched over
with my sap slowly rising,
and I am the swallow flying
in a peach-colored canyon,
the roan deer running,
and the dancing snow.

But I am also the baby
with a thorn in my back,
the deafening crash,
and the suffering beast,
and sometimes I am
the girl letting go.

I encountered a man I had been engaged to decades before, and was confronted with the life that could have been.

Discarded Lover

When I saw you today,
after so many years,
your face so changed,
your eyes so familiar,
I felt in that single stab of time
a lifetime of unmade memories—
the pictures on the mantle never taken,
your boys   now men
who've forgotten my name.

Like life inhaled and never released.

Now time has roared over me
like a tornado of a million precious leaves,
and I have lived the circular sameness of years
with few memories to mark the time,
only to find myself here,
kneeling in these crumbling leaves
in the canted, autumn light,
a kind horse nudging me for food,
it's warm breath
evaporating upward.

In this poem, I challenged myself to write in a traditional, rhyming form. Dedicated to my dogs, Jasper and Tucker.

Ode to a Dog

You are the flash of trout in a stream,
the apogee of a ball in the sky,
all the innocent, unworded things—
the sideways, beckoning gleam of eye.

You revel in the tender grass,
sniff a hundred worlds upon the wind,
a lifetime's joy in a second's pass—
your ecstatic leap as the ball descends.

I think eighty years too long to live,
when ten or twelve of yours would do,
to live a life of innocence
while all the world is fresh and new.

I used to live on a ranch in the Napa Valley where the landlords kept a menagerie of animals. That ranch was burned in the Glass Fire of 2020. This poem is in memory of that land and the animals who perished in the fire.

The Ranch at Dusk

I am very popular with the hummingbirds,
the cats, however, are skeptical,
and the geese despise me.
The goats are opportunists,
they appraise me with alien eyes,
chewing like machines
on the olive branch I offer.
If I were to ask them for a favor,
I am sure they would claim
they never knew me.

The donkeys look forlorn,
they push their velvet muzzles
through gaps in the fence
and condescend
to chew on my apple
only if I cut it into pieces.
But at least

they huff at me in thanks
as I walk away.

The emus cock their wrinkled heads
from side to side,
discerning from a distance
what I hold in my hand—
overripe plums,
sunflower seeds,
I don't quite know
what they want.

I have read that
emus are related to dinosaurs.

Sometimes in the darkening dusk,
I approach them
with no food in my hand.
We are primitive beasts
in primordial light.
I cock my head at them,
they thrum deep in their bellies,
and finally
allow me
to stroke
their
long,
feathered
necks.

An homage to the Napa Valley.

I Know These Trees

I know these trees,
this draping leaf and canted rock.
I've breathed this manzanita wind,
walked upon this crunch of soil
birthing budding vines.

This golden, guilty land,
a wild horse broken.
This frontier so lately found,
so
      finally
            won.

Picture this western land
a thousand years ago—
thirty million thundering bison,
skies darkened with pigeons,
a few humans
gathering water,
collecting acorns,
building homes of willow bark.

I sometimes wish
this new world had never been found,
that those pompous, masted ships
had veered off course,

and it were wild still.

*One of those moments that happens in a blink
and stays with you.*

Thirty Seconds at a Stoplight

So much time on my hands
since retirement   I am
as gladly forgotten as
these dusty weeds growing
out of the pavement
by the side of the highway.
But they have their burst of life,
such as it is.

A stooped woman dodders by
with her ancient, tear-stained poodle.
He appears to be blind and missing a leg,
but still   wagging.
A mud-caked tennis ball lies
in the weeds by the curb.
Whose hands have touched it?
What exuberant bounce
it once had,
for a short while the hero of some game,
some momentary racking of points.

I cannot look anywhere these days
without seeing a poem.

A letter in poem form to a childhood friend with whom I went on great adventures into the New England woods as a kid.

Letter to a Childhood Friend

As for me,
I am living tucked away
beside a forgotten vineyard,
the vines grown shaggy and fruitless,
misshapen,
thirsty for attention.

You are right, my old friend,
we know nothing of ourselves.
Our bodies age like withered grapes
still clinging to the vine,
while our minds continue asking
the questions of children,
the answers always begging more questions
until we give up asking.

How about you, old friend?
Remember when we inhabited bodies
that sparked like fireflies
and our dreams rang out like church bells?
Remember when we thought life would answer us?

I feel as if I am ever trying
to gather up the years in my arms
like a great bundle of dry leaves,
but the more I pick up,
the more fall from my grasp,
until I have given up entirely
and let them all blow away in a spiral wind.

And you
Have you come to terms with the years?
or like me,
is the core of you,
the green apple core of you,
still staring in wonder
at a speckled sparrow's egg
or a cluster of ripe berries
in a brambly wood?

Apologies to all the lovely men out there that don't fit this stereotype. I just couldn't resist.

Farewell Speech to the Human Male

Too bad you couldn't
adjust.
We kept you around
as long as
we could.
We liked the way you
smelled,
your strong, hairy
chests,
your tight grip on
mayonnaise jars,
your comic relief,
but you were just too
problematic.

Disagreements turned into aggression,
(always with the aggression,)
the entitlement,
the inability to
decorate or
emote.
It was too much,

or perhaps
too little.

Our wombs had the final
say.
We sent you all to another
planet
to huff and puff among yourselves,
shipping the sperm back
via space drone
upon request.

I had two homes burn down in California
wildfires over a three-year period. I suppose I am
an accidental Buddhist, having been so harshly
confronted with the impermanence of things.

Wildfire Elegy

I used to think I could rely on the days,
one following the other like panting dogs,
the expectant breath of morning,
the folding limbs of night,
the years tumbling by like floodwaters.

Nature's mood is generally predictable like that,
except for the periodic cataclysm—
a meteor annihilating the dinosaurs,
tectonic plates colliding
and depositing a mountain range.
But you never think of a cataclysm interrupting
your own placid days.
You never think
        you
            are the dinosaur.

You never think about how
you are just carbon rearranged,
something combustible,
how all the treasures

16

you've collected in a lifetime
are just more fuel to a flame—
that delicate painting of yellow poppies
I hung on the wall wherever I lived,
consumed as greedily
as a forgotten sock under my bed.

My mother's thumb-stained recipes,
a lover's penciled poem,
that nut-brown guitar that played a thousand songs,
the carefully-tended jasmine,
my old cowboy boots still stained
with the sweat of my youth,
even
my mother's ashes that rested on a shelf,
now twice burned,
mingle in the rubble.

Now I no longer belong to a place.
The objects that housed my memories
have combusted.
I alone am left to remember the things,
when I thought the things would be left
to remember me.

Inspired by a story I read about a Muslim lady
lamenting her life as a woman.

Collect My Dust

God
when I die
collect my dust
but do not remake me a woman
make of me a stone
a rock reposing on the lap of the earth
unnoticed
elemental
resplendent in the cold moonlight
empty of utterance
of no particular use
except perhaps
to toss into the sea
one ecstatic splash
the only word I speak

The next two poems came from an exercise in writing from "prompts." The first prompt was- "Write a poem about clouds." The second prompt was- "Begin a poem with the words- 'Water does not flow.'"

The Space Between

They're always wanting sun,
waiting for it to
come out
(as if it ever left!)
pleased with a forecast
of uninterrupted light.
But I am like the rain
intermittent,
precipitant,
thirty percent chance of
deluges of silence,
drizzles of uncertainty,
sprinkles of regret.

But today I caught myself
considering the space between
clouds,
closed my eyes,
and waited.

Flow

Water does not flow
only when it's told to,
or stop to wonder if
it deserves to flow,
or question if flowing
is appropriate,
or expect to hear applause
as it races by.

Water does not flow backward,
only forward
               always
                    forward.

When winter comes
and no options remain,
it is not a failure
to freeze,
but a cumulation of energy,
a season of stillness to gather
strength   enough
to melt
and flow
a new course.

I moved into a retirement community in 2021 which inspired this poem.

On Retirement

We have lived and lived and lived some more,
stacked up the years in snapshot rows,
(almost aghast at life's generosity)
wiped the children,
fed the husbands,
sat half-masted
at the desk
until the numbers added up.

Now pardoned   we
lounge in
modular homes
stacked side by side like
preliminary coffins,
finally sitting still
long enough to notice
a barely-open apple blossom,
a squirrel tap-dancing on the roof,
a stranger's poem.

But
they say— don't sit *too* still,

we must be nimble
we must be quick!
remember our memory exercises,
do our strength training
so we can die strong.

But I wonder,
does a spent flower try to gather
its petals?
And how does a flying bird die?
Does it fall from the sky?

The following three poems were inspired by my
relationship with technology.

I Am Not a Robot

Today my computer asked me
to confirm my humanity
by clicking an icon.
Is that what passes for being human now?
I'd rather prove I'm human
by laughing or
singing or
falling
in love
or
crying or
screaming or
falling out of love,
but I guess that's
so twentieth-century of me.

As for being human,
I'm beginning to wonder.

I click the icon
just to be sure.

Suspicious Spam

Thirty years ago when I was thirty,
suspicious spam was
a tin of processed meat
that smelled funny.
Now,
it is the lens of cynicism
I view the world through
in a daily struggle
to maintain trust in humanity.

Every other call
on my cell phone flashes—
SUSPECTED SPAM,
ninety percent of the junk
in my mailbox gets tossed,
half of my emails
come disguised as Promotions,
even the nice men who come by
to fix the plumbing
pressure me to sign up for their
Rewards Club and try to overcharge me.
(or is that a suspicious *scam*?)

Text **STOP**
BLOCK number
CLEAR your cookies
Press 9 to **END THIS CALL!**

#13,017

I try to be
a unique, creative soul,
an agent of good,
a witness to beauty,
but I fear
the cold, hard truth is
the world views me as
a taxpayer ID number,
a consumer entity,
potential sale #13, 017
on some bot's cold call list.

I imagine myself rising to heaven
on wings of glory
the day I die
and turning to take
one last, wistful look
at the earth below
only to see
the entire face of the planet
obliterated by a gigantic neon sign
flashing one final message for me:

"Thank You For Shopping With Us!"

The Disappearance of Things

Every day something disappears—
my waist
        my hair
                my chin.

Every day something is lost—
that actor's name, *you* know…
my third google password,
my cell phone   again.

Every day something changes—
she is now they,
your is now ur,
hi is now hey.

I used to think I was not old yet,
and fairly hip,
but   apparently
I am
full of it.

A Shakespearean Sonnet

A thousand thoughts lying within
A hundred thousand if I say true
Breath'd to life by ink and pen
If only I could yet construe
The purpose of these tangl'd words
Once safely packed away inside
Granted flight like cage'd birds
Who only seek a place to hide
Making poetry of childhood trauma
Disappointments, memories
Forcing rhymes of life's old drama
Editing the tragedies
I'll gather them like children, perhaps
And settle them down for long, winter's naps.

I Will Arise and Go Now (à la Yeats)

I will arise and go now
to the bathroom late at night,
and stumble on the lying dog,
and fumble with the light.

And I shall have some peace there,
but peace comes dripping slow,
where midnight's all a shiver
'cause the heater's set too low.

I will go back to bed now,
back to my queen-size reckoning,
hoping sleep alights with angel's wings
where dreams of youth are beckoning.

This poem that came in fits and starts one night
as I was trying to sleep. I woke myself many
times to write down the phrases. The next
morning, I constructed this poem.

Inconsolable Beauty

I float face up in the pool
    suspended,
my arms splayed like a crucifix.
A hummingbird flits over me.
A jet soars thirty thousand feet above.
Is that not a miracle?
and me, floating?

What awful joy is life,
what inconsolable beauty.
Eight billion crashing souls
spilling hailstorms of words,
we pace ahead of ourselves,
irreverent, strident beings,
imagining ourselves deserving
    when
the depth of mercy we owe
each other is withheld.

And you,
(there is always a you)
who didn't love enough
who didn't give enough.
But floating here,
I realize
it was I
who held too tightly to my heart.

How can I contain it all?
the pleading animal eyes,
the disappointed lovers,
the barely-cloaked resentments of children,
the barking foxes,
the wild finches,
the night-blooming jasmine.

The universe screams inside me.

Our hearts clash like sparks of God
flinting off each other,
floating like wayward angels
in an infinite storm of beauty.

This poem arose from a desire to escape humanity's inhumanity.

Reptilian Dream

If I could shed these clothes,
pluck out this hair,
retract these too-long arms,
curve these fingers into claws,
shrink my eyes to yellow orbs,
I'd snake-shed this human form,
live like a wild, wizened thing
who nestles in the roots of trees
and speaks the language of bumblebees.
I'd dart my eyes, flick my tongue,
warm my cold blood in the sun,
and know a kind of joy.

I tried to convey a sense of waiting in this poem.

After You Left

Three roses float in a bowl,
the lightest shade of pink
before it becomes white,
like the inside of a seashell.

The white dog waits by the door.
The black cat sleeps on the yellow chair.
The pale curtains breathe like gills
at the barely-cracked window.

I never knew you could hear
a rose petal fall on water.

Morning Tea

I went out early
to drink my tea
in the garden.
The dog was
besotted with the scent
of a dandelion.
A hummingbird sipped
from a bottlebrush bush.
A flock of wild geese
flew over so low,
I heard the whoosh of their wings.
At my feet I saw
a crumple of earth
left by a diligent gopher.

There are many worlds
in this world:

the dog,
peeing the parameters
of his territory
for the thousandth time.

The hummingbirds
enforce a complex government
in that bottlebrush bush,
an ongoing war of nectar and pistils.

The wild geese,
intent on keeping formation,
are urged south
by a magnetic pinpoint in their brain,
a world of flyways
and windways and water.

And the gopher
what of him?
His underground labyrinths,
his furious digging,
a mastermind of dirt   he is
compelled by things
I cannot comprehend.

I smile to think
each one   including me,
views the world as their own,
with themselves
at its center.

We must remember each other.

Layers

I feel the soft decay
of our aging souls,
a gentle cynicism
life has impaled on us.
And yet   there
across the kitchen table
is your boyish smile,
comfortable as an old slipper,
that saucy spark in your rumpled eyes,
the timbre of your voice unchanged,
your *I love you* as soft as rain.

I see now
you are a pink-cheeked boy
in an old man's body and
I am a six-year-old girl
in drag.

Beneath our onion layers of years
we are still children,
eager for love
and waiting for Christmas.

In Other Words

Everyone
tells their soul's poem
with whatever language they have.

My friend Juan
loves to run
and run
and run.
His pace is his rhythm,
the race is his poem.

My neighbor Marge
is always cooking up some
sugary, crispy concoction.
She writes her poem in
syllables of cinnamon.

That woman at the gym
who swims for hours,
slices through the water
like a sleek metaphor.

And you, sleeping
in a hyphen of moonlight,
the semi-colon of your shoulder
where it meets your neck
is sublime.

This poem extols the beauty of the natural world,
but also asks—What will happen if humanity
doesn't come to its senses and save it?

What Then

If not for the evening light split by a wintry branch,
if not for the golden plain of a lover's thigh,
if not for the midnight anthem of wild geese,
but what of the starving child's lullaby?
The trouble that hones you down
like a ham in a smokehouse,
sucking up your fat,
dripping you dry?

If not for the embryonic hymn of ocean tides,
if not for its chant of ancient song,
if not for the stippled sand
and whispering grass,
but what of the slick of oil
and the beached
whale's gasp?

What of the river's drip and the willow weeping?
What of the proud, unrighteous men?
When poets run out of words
and put down their pens,
if so   I ask
what then?

I end with this poem, tongue-in-cheek.

Not Again

The night I died,
an angel came to me
and asked—
"What did you do with the life
you were given?"

"Well,"
I said,
"I mopped the floor,
washed the car,
walked the dog,
made the bed,
changed the oil,
scrubbed the toilet,
washed the dishes,
watered the plants,
folded the laundry,
cleaned the gutters,
rebooted the computer,
opened the mail,
paid the bills,
filled the tank,
raked the leaves,
packed boxes,

cooked the meals,
unpacked boxes,
made deposits,
made withdrawals
and after all that
I only had enough time left
to write this stupid poem."

"In that case," the shining angel said,
"you shall be granted
another lifetime to
do it all again,
but next time you must find a way
to write more poems."

"Not again!" I cried.

But the angel just winked at me
and flew away.

Made in the USA
Monee, IL
24 September 2023

43239739R00025